USBORNE FIRST READING
Level Four

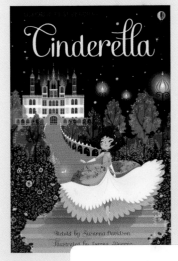

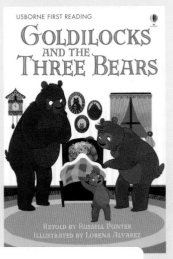

The Elves
and the
Shoemaker

Rob Lloyd Jones

Illustrated by John Joven

Reading consultant: Alison Kelly

Once there was a shoemaker.
All day long, he sat at a
workbench in his shoe shop.

Years ago, he had made wonderful shoes. They were admired far and wide. But things had changed...

The shoemaker had grown old. His back ached and his fingers hurt from stitching tough leather.

He no longer made such
wonderful shoes. No one
wanted to buy them.

He only had enough money
to make one more pair.

The shoemaker's wife saw
how tired he was. "Make them
in the morning," she said.

So the shoemaker left the
shoe leather on his workbench
and went to bed.

The next morning, he had a big surprise. There, on the bench, were...

And what *magnificent* shoes!
They were sleek and shiny
and perfectly stitched.

The shoemaker sold them the moment he opened his shop.

Now, he could afford leather to make two pairs of shoes.

He left the leather on his workbench and went to bed.

In the morning, two pairs of boots stood there.

The shoemaker sold
them in minutes.

What lovely
laces!

Now he could afford leather
for *four* pairs of shoes.

Again, he left the leather on his workbench. Again, new shoes appeared overnight.

Every morning, for several weeks, the shoemaker found new shoes on his workbench. They had shiny buckles...

twirly ribbons...

...and fancy bows.

Every day, the shoemaker and his wife sold the new shoes in their shop.

Handsome heels!

Splendid slippers!

Now, everyone wanted the shoemaker's shoes.

But the shoemaker felt bad. They were not really *his* shoes. Someone else had done all the work.

"Let's hide in the workshop tonight," his wife suggested. "We can see who is making the shoes."

That night, the shop door
creaked open. Soft feet
padded across the floor.

Two tiny figures sprang up
onto the workbench.

"Elves?" gasped the shoemaker's wife.

The little creatures were barefoot and wore only rags.

The elves grinned and giggled. They found some shoe leather, and a needle and thread.

Then they began to work.

They worked so fast, their
hands were a blur. The whole
time they laughed and sang.

Finally, the elves leaped
from the bench and rushed
out into the dawn light.

"Elves..." the shoemaker muttered.

"Elves?" his wife said again.

"ELVES!" they cried together.

It seemed impossible,
but the new shoes proved
it was real.

That day, the shoe shop
was busier than ever, but the
shoemaker kept thinking
about the elves.

"I must make something for
them in return," he said. "But
what can I make that they
might want?"

That afternoon, the
shoemaker sat at his
workbench and he worked.

His back ached and his fingers hurt. But he kept on working until moonlight shone through the shop window.

He placed what he had
made on the bench. Then he
hid again with his wife.

The elves sneaked silently
into the shop.

When they saw the
shoemaker's gift they
squealed with joy.

The little suits were finer
than anything worn by lords
or ladies or kings or queens.

What happy little elves are we,
no longer workmen shall we be.

Delightedly, the elves
danced around the bench,
admiring their new suits.

Finally, they skipped out
of the door and into the silver
moonlight.

We look so fine in our new suits,

no longer shall we stitch new boots.

The shoemaker and his wife never saw the elves again, or knew why the creatures had helped them.

But now they had enough
money to live comfortably for
the rest of their lives.

And so they did.

About the story

The Elves and the Shoemaker was first written down, around 200 years ago, by Jacob and Wilhelm Grimm. The Grimm brothers collected lots of fairy tales, including *Cinderella* and *Snow White*.

Designed by Laura Nelson
Series designer: Russell Punter
Series editor: Lesley Sims

First published in 2016 by Usborne Publishing Ltd.,
Usborne House, 83-85 Saffron Hill, London EC1N 8RT, England.
www.usborne.com Copyright © 2016 Usborne Publishing Ltd.

USBORNE FIRST READING
Level Four

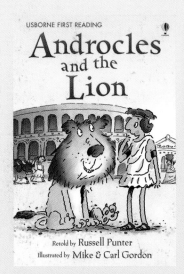

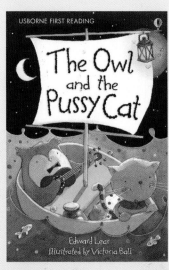

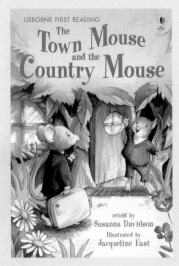

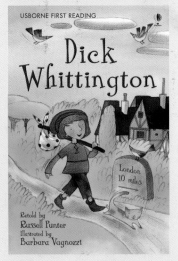